HEY DUGGEE

A DAY AT THE BEACH

MEET DUGGEE.

He is a great big cuddly dog. Duggee is in charge
of all the fun and adventures at the clubhouse.

Would you like to meet Duggee's Squirrel Club?

NORRIE
is a kind
mouse.

BETTY
is a clever
octopus.

TAG
is a gentle
rhino.

ROLY
is a noisy
little hippo.

HAPPY
is a very happy
crocodile!

There is always something to do at Duggee's Clubhouse.
What will it be this time?

It's a lovely day, so Duggee has brought everyone to the beach.

Duggee has even brought Enid the cat!
Can you spot her?

Everyone is enjoying themselves.
The chickens are relaxing . . .

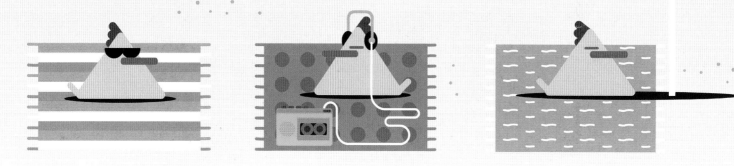

Frog is keeping cool . . .

Enid is wondering how the sea works . . .

. . . and Duggee is having a little lie-down. Aaaah-woof!

Roly is very busy in the sand.

"DIG! DIG! DIG!
DIG! DIG! DIG!"

"DIG! DIG! DIG!"

"I made a sandcastle!" he says.

"It looks more like a sand hill," says Betty.

Oh dear. Roly didn't see Duggee there!

"Can you help us make a sandcastle, Duggee?" asks Norrie.

Duggee knows what to do.
He has his **SANDCASTLE BADGE.**

How do you make a sandcastle?
Get a bucket and spade.

Dig up some wet sand.

Remember to pat it down.

Pour it into your bucket.

Tip your bucket
upside down.

Now LIFT.
Ta-dah!

A sandcastle!

"Let's make a BIGGER ONE!" says Roly.

"YAY!" say the other Squirrels.

Meanwhile, further up the beach . . .

PECK!
PECK!

PECK!

Do you mind?

"Nigel. **NIGEL!**" calls Mr Crab. Nigel wakes up too.

POP!

"Every day I get woken up by a seagull, Nigel," says Mr Crab. "We have got to find a new place to live."

PAT! PAT! PAT!

What's that noise? Mr Crab and Nigel go to have a look.

"Oh, such quality work!" says Mr Crab.
"Would you make a new home for us?"

"Would we?" the Squirrels ask Duggee.
"A-woof!" nods Duggee.

"Yay!" cheer the Squirrels.

"Yay!" cheers Mr Crab.

Norrie makes some plans.

Tag makes a wall.

Roly makes a ....

"WINDOW!"

Tag makes a garden.

Happy makes a pond.

Roly makes some . . .

"STAIRS!"

And Betty adds some finishing touches. All done!

"Oh, Nigel!" says Mr Crab. "Isn't it wonderful?"

Let's see what's inside!

Great big windows.

A fridge-freezer.

A hall, decorated with shells.

A fireplace.

A piano!

The Squirrels have even made . . .

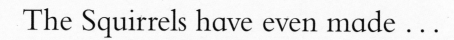

. . . a roof terrace! Amazing!

"Thank you, Squirrels," says Mr Crab. "We love it!"

Haven't the Squirrels done well today!
They've earned their . . .

SANDCASTLE BADGE!

 cheer the Squirrels. There's just time for one more
thing before the Squirrels go home.

"DUGGEE HUG!"

"Let's enjoy this, Nigel . . .

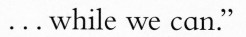

. . . while we can."

Can you earn your Sandcastle Badge? Do these activities, then write your name on the next page and ask an adult to help you cut it out.

Can you visit a sandpit or beach and make a sandcastle?

Crabs have shells. What other things have shells?

If you were making a castle for Mr Crab, what would you put in it?

What else can you do in the sand? Make a picture? Make a sand person?

Mr Crab walks sideways. Walk sideways, like a crab.

Sometimes people put a flag on top of a sandcastle. Draw a flag and decorate it.

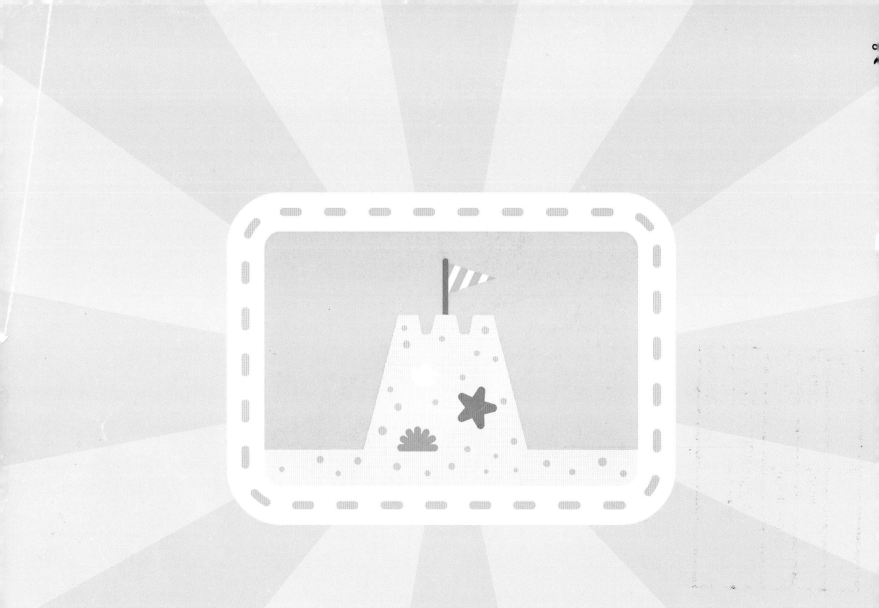

earned their
SANCASTLE BADGE